You Have Reached the End of the Future

You Have Reached the End of the Future

A collection of new poems by Hwang Inchan
Translated by Hoyoung Moon

K

아시아

Contents

YOU HAVE REACHED THE END OF THE FUTURE

Pa-wuh

I wandered through the mountain all day in
search of the pig let loose to search for mushrooms
This wasn't in my living hours

Just a dream act

Mushrooms or pigs or mountains I don't really
care for but why do they appear in my dreams
Why do I write them into poems

And yet I was awake all night

Lost in the mountain I stood in deep forest The
sun hadn't even risen and yet

Somewhere a bird stirred from sleep began to cry

All around me bird-cries filled the air

CheeecheeeppippippOinnnkoinkoink

The birds couldn't be seen nor the pig found

In any case, amidst the chorus of living things

everything except me seemed connected as one

That was a dream too

Outside of dreams, this is what happens for

instance

I was in the mountains holding a weapon in order
to guard some weapons Another person in the
mountain holding a weapon to guard the weapons
with me was to tell me an important truth

But this being the darkest hour before dawn I'd
slipped into sleep And the dream I dreamt then
was the pigmushroom dream

In the dawn air and light where all is wrapped in
silence
 he smiled looking at me stirred from sleep
 and told me the important truth, but I knew this

was not what he had meant to say

Traffic

At the crossroads the duck crossed I realized this
was no one's fault

I wasn't the only one who had this revelation
Watching the duck go by
    it came to everyone's mind

No one knew what it was, but still
    understood something

There goes the duck Ducks cry as they walk
Quack quack it cries as it walks

    Waddle waddle it plods

It's sad when ducks cry

But the duck isn't sad

Over and over someone cries As they walk they
cry

Light

—You call things beautiful so easily

—Is that a bad thing

You respond without looking at the screen

It's spring there I think you said You must be
looking out the window or something You said you
could see the cherry blossoms in full bloom I talked
about the lab animals who got pregnant, and you
had called that beautiful

—What are you looking at

—Nothing

To my right the antarctic sea lies open Full of white or blue sometimes all this feels like a scene from a dream It's been too long since I talked to you in person

—When you come back, why don't we go see the ocean?

—It's all ice and ocean here, what do you mean go see the ocean

We talked The botanical garden and the gallery, the beach and the park, places we'd been but wanted to visit again, things we wanted to see there again But conversation always breaks around here, and outside is a world of negative 37 degrees Celsius

I get up and look outside All scenery I already know

—Is that a bad thing

—Nothing

—When you come back, why don't we go see the ocean?

In the screen you were talking without me

Was it really cherry blossoms you were looking at then, I will never know now

Hunting Prohibited

"No hunting Hunting isn't allowed You mustn't hunt ever"

Why did a small rabbit say this to me
The rabbit stood in the middle of the street

Hunting is scary,
Hunting is bad,

With that the rabbit flared its nostrils and scratched its ear with a hind paw pretending to be distracted

How adorable

This was the sort of thought I had as I watched
the rabbit

I was hunted

No one knew why there was a small rabbit
standing in the middle of the street

Before the Law

I walked a long road to reach Heaven and arrived at its door guarded by an angel and a sword of flame

The door opens and a child poking its head out asks
Is Heaven here?

I wait with the guard in front of the door Til Heaven gone makes its way back

Loss of Sight

Why do people plant trees indoors?

It's a weekend morning crowded with empty
chairs that embarrass me

Sagging tree limbs unable to bear the weight of
leaves
Shapes that are called beautiful shapes

With all my might
I am focusing on an embarrassing task

Bringing in a single chair, emptying that chair
Excuse me, when a voice echoes in the room no

one is in

it gets more embarrassing in a way

Tree limbs that don't stop at sagging, they lay down roots

But why is it that people plant trees indoors?
The leaves are very blue-green and glossy as well

And I have heard when an indoor tree exhibits growth on its own it is someone's providence

Who said so?
That this would make everything better, who said

that?

The leaves are so blue-green and heavy and yearn
toward ground
they glower a strange presence

I try to believe it's a slight troublesome misunder-
standing that often occurs in the morning hours

But how should I ask?
Why people plant trees indoors, why those trees
grow however they like
and acquire more empty chairs, about those
wooden objects that eventually, in proportion,

embarrass me

Glasses

The sea swallows the glasses

Afraid, I walk straight ahead
Push-pulled by the water, barely standing

Glasses, go find the glasses
Need to find them

Walking in water, soon you can't see any-
one the sea disappears fear evaporates

Glasses
Only the glasses remain

I walk straight ahead

Glasses clasped tight

Evening Bell

Lots of people were waiting for the bell to be rung
Fireworks exploded Shouts and cheers could be
heard

Let's go somewhere, anywhere now

I was grateful for those words Above our heads
uncountable things are falling The bell had at some
point

stopped ringing

People walked Past the river banks Past Han River
Past other people who had already died

They were walking the new year

People kept walking on Past the crumbled
apartments Past the spindly trees lining the street
Let's go somewhere, anywhere now

Merciful, useless words

Bells echoed through the air again The new year
began in the middle of the night

White Acts / One Hundred Lines

Atop the desk was a bundle of half-written novel drafts and a potted cactus that had yellowed, in front of the desk was my beloved

"How could you? Poets, the lot of you…"

As he spoke I was watching a live spider slowly, busily eat another spider alive

He said he would quit now
But he didn't say what he was quitting

The spider was slowly sucking something out of the spider wrapped in its silk He said he was going to go horseback riding

He would slowly ride a white horse around the
tracks, he said
(And he was going to quit, he stressed once more)

The spiderhouse was getting rained on but the
spider didn't move

These were all words written in a book

I understand everything you're going to do, I said
I understand, I said

Let's Not Laugh Too Loudly

Yeonnam-dong at night is full of people Dogs too,
but even more people than dogs

But
when I think of the people I walked the night
streets of Yeonnam-dong with

I'm not sure who to picture first

Though I clearly remember walking with people
I can't tell apart past people walking with their dog
or other people

Stores appear then disappear

Who knows what kind of store

Each time it's really delicious but actually a little
too salty and actually too expensive although Wow,
this is really good, I remember saying but thinking
there was no way I would come here twice

The decent stores disappear so quickly
People would grumble, and thinking of them

I'm not sure who to picture first

A little walk from Yeonnam-dong is Hongdae
A little walk from there is Yeonhee-dong But I

couldn't go anywhere Crumpled in Yeonnam-
dong watching the passerby with no end This I
remember but

Who are those people I walked the night streets of
Yeonnam-dong with
Are you alive

I am for now
If you are also…

That alone is enough to make me happy

Happiness makes Light and Light is the Word

thus the Word may create humans

Yet Yeonnam-dong in the morning isn't as crowded as I expected

That I learned this time

Jigukchong Jigukchong

I went to the lake with my love When we rowed
the water made a sound

Jigukchong jigukchong uhsawa[*]

I had no idea that was the sound from rowing
My love chuckled over and over like it was a funny
incident

But what's so funny
I couldn't quite understand and when I rowed

---

[*] A transliteration of the line "至匊悤 至匊悤 於思臥" from the classical
Korean poem 어부사시사 (漁夫四時詞, Four Seasons of a Fisherman's
Life) by Yoon Seondo. A sijo written in 1651, 어부사시사 is often taught
in high-school level Korean literature classes, and the line appears as an
onomatopoeic refrain depicting the sound of oars against water.

I could hear the water

I was in the fog with my love The lake was so quiet
I felt afraid somehow

Why does my love keep laughing

Jigukchong jigukchong uhsawa

The sounds that didn't quite sound like that echoed and overlapped with laughter

The fog was so thick I couldn't see anything but

the two of us

I think we should go back

I meant to shout

But no sounds came out

The Day the Hat Disappeared

There was an endless line of people at the Ueno
Zoo waiting to see the pandas As if they'd stayed
alive this long just to see the pandas

In the classroom after classes had ended
the kid told me so

But there was no occasion where we went to the
zoo together In this poem the sort of thing you are
thinking does not happen

I saw a white cat on the street I saw a black dog
see it and bark This too does not mean the sort of
thing you are thinking

Midsummer night,

the zoo sold panda hats I heard

and the way back on my own

is a narrow alley

Nothing to be seen except my lengthening

shadow

The missing hat hasn't returned yet

That bears no relation to what you are thinking

Shatterproof

Rain falls

When I start a poem like this it's like I've already
finished the poem

When I start a poem by talking about poetry
it's like I've managed to write something

The way talking about love
makes you feel a little more in love

But what should happen after the rain falls?

Whether to talk about the rain, or describe two
people in the rain, the smell of dirt on rainy days or

the heavy damp sensation of wet clothes, as I mull

Rain falls
Once I've written that down I feel relieved

"Work going okay?"

When you asked, the darkness of night was approaching outside the window, and now that the outdoors have darkened the window reflects what's inside

There you see two people facing each other in the soft and cozy atmosphere, choosing their words carefully because there is so much to say

I should leave things at that today,
I come to think as I watch your face

We smile and stand side by side at the door

There is someone knocking on the door
Someone drenched in rain

Someone calling me

Infinitude

Janghee doesn't fall asleep but thinks of the bear at the zoo Janghee likes bears best out of all animals Why do you like bears the most? When Mom asks, there is no response, just rrrawr rrrawr Now mother is no more but the bear remains

In a fairytale, a hunter chased a bear to its cave but decided not to hunt it upon seeing a young bear there, and since then that land has been called Young Bear In another story two bears bit and killed forty-two children who mocked the prophet, and in another story a bear becomes human and gives birth to a child

Janghee's favorite story of all

is the story of the bear who doesn't hibernate in winter

Because the bear doesn't go to sleep when it should there is chaos in the forest The birds and stars and trees and winds they all fret and fuss until eventually the bear leaves the forest and clambers into the cold winter

Bear is sad Janghee doesn't fall asleep

Bear's sadness seeps out of the zoo and fills the city

A rainy winter night

When the whole world is steeped in sadness

Janghee barely, finally falls asleep thinking of the

bear

That is how this story begins

The Shakes

If you keep the window open on a rainy day the
indoors get drenched

Guess I should sleep on the floor today,
he says with a smile

Lying on the living room floor, he imagined
A world where the ground shakes Trees shake
Buildings shake so everything crumples

Falling to the ground side by side Two people
Two trees
Two animals' limbs

They'll fall

asleep

Upon waking everything is different

Relationships made new
The indoors made new

Everything exchanges each other

Outside the window the streets have already dried
white, all the buildings look more vivid than ever,

and he believes this is truly love

Did you sleep well? He asks me,

and I ask, Did something happen yesterday

Yeah, no, he replies with a smile

Scentless

Two feet are walking

Scentless feet

I came to have very large white feet

Without any suspicious smells

or heady scents, without anything like that

can I really live well?

Without a trace

without any heart

two feet walk side by side

Something like a dog's pawprints is left behind

Phantasming Film

Watching the countless rays falling outside the
window
makes me think this can't be reality

I see a playground dried to a crisp
I see kids running

From here everything is a bit whiter
and fuzzier than I thought

What was it that I thought…

I walked the dark hallways for a long while
Afraid of running into someone I know

If this were a film I would have run into someone,
a teacher who was fond of me when I was little,
or that kid all grown up

Outside, the kids are shouting something

The hallways are so cold that I feel relieved
Rather than unexpected joy, the familiarity of
sadness puts me at ease

Watching the countless rays falling outside the
window
makes me think this can't be real life

I walked the dark hallways for a long while

Putting my chilled hands in my pockets warmed

them up a bit

Metronome

I come home with a child whose hair has turned white over the day
A black army trailing behind the child

Birds perched atop the bell tower fly away
Cheep cheep the sounds of military boots echo round

What's left is the alleyway of iron doors

Doors that haven't been opened

Waking Hour

I should not put any more dreams in poems

If I put what happens in dreams in poems it becomes reality Sand fairies or pale horses These things are already a dime a dozen in the streets

Mid-meal he spoke
It was such a strange thing to say I couldn't even ask what he was talking about

"Life's really tough lately, isn't it?" (Words chosen after much deliberation)

The moment morning light descends and lingers

at the dining table

　and everything is set in place like a still life
painting or a shot from a movie

　The thought that there's always a bird chirping in
scenes like this
　The thought that our lives strive a bit excessively
toward a mise-en-scéne Around the time this occurs
to me

　I realize this is a dream I've had before

　He's eating a meal no one has prepared
　A white horse closes its eyes in the living room light

You Have Reached the End of the Future

At lunch everyone's tied up They go somewhere
for a while and come back shortly

One takes a walk
Another falls in the water

People keep wandering the outskirts of the park
and that is the life of moderns I see I understand

But this has no relation to understanding I
understand that as well

Lovers breaking up under the mild light of
afternoon Serious, sad faces they have They're

anticipating the freedom post-separation

It's not like we can go somewhere other than the
park but…

The walks continue
Because at lunch everyone's tied up

The person who fell in the water is walking out of
the water now

POET'S NOTES

POET

A Thrice-Repeated Story

1

What is the act of writing? What is poetry? And what is the act of writing poetry? When I think of things like this, I find myself at a loss. Someone said poetry is a free thing but what I find there is only confinement and the premonition of confinement. A bird is not free. A bird is only as free as it has been permitted. Just as a cage without the bird is freedom to Gim Choon-soo, poetry's confinements appear to me as freedom. What we see is not the freedom of poetry but the dream of freedom a poem dreams, and even that we cannot touch or see properly. Poetry that dreams of infinite freedom is beautiful but it is beautiful because it is useless and impossible. Like others, I am drawn to its uselessness.

So one writes in desperation. As a prisoner, here in this darkness, I dream of the glittering outdoors. What my hand touches is the cold, firm wall, but as I look at it I imagine the light and air on the other side. Without having seen or known freedom, I believe that is freedom, that freedom is there. The way darkness alludes to light, and a life of suffering points to peace in the aftermath, poetry's confinements will reveal its freedom. That is what I believe.

Maybe being aware of one's confinement is one of the most concrete ways of being aware of one's presence here. It will be the most powerful weapon that pierces through our world and flies toward freedom on the other side. The finer our confinement, and the more acutely we are aware of it, the better we can approach true freedom, that impossibility.

Therefore I write. I write that which points to freedom while in confinement, yet clearly cannot arrive at freedom; that which one cannot know altogether, not exactly. That nebulous thing called poetry.

2

Beholding an object makes it disappear. The moment one chooses an object it escapes the position of the beheld. This is the mystery of writing. Writing about something only rarifies it, only widens the distance. A poem always fails without having met its object; if we really want to hold on to the object we should give up the act of writing. Otherwise what we grasp and hold up will only be our humble desires. But these small, petty desires are probably the driving force that keeps us going at the useless act that is poetry. What a tedious exercise, where you can't win freedom or reach your object! One might as well say the act of writing is always preceded by the qualifier "despite".

What can one say about an object one cannot capture? I can only muster the effort to say it exists or doesn't. And even if I've said so, I know that doesn't mean the object is truly present or absent. Poetry is a failure of the object, so the act of stating that the object is present or not also only arrives at failure.

When we write about the object, it cannot be held in place; it endlessly ebbs and flows between presence and absence; it is merely found leaning toward one side at a certain moment. Here, being and not being don't denounce each other. Like shades of brightness, it appears as an infinite number of possibilities between black and white. The object is a little bit present and a little bit absent.

All objects are gray. One could also make such a declaration. The object can be infinitely close to black or infinitely close to white, but it is gray, in the end. Neither clear-cut victory nor loss, it is endlessly delayed; it's dead yet alive while it hasn't died or lived, like Schrodinger's cat; until the definitive moment comes, these states coexist. An eternal state of suspension lies between us and the object as an abyss we cannot cross.

Despite this, we continue to write. Of objects that grow ever so rarified, ever so distanced from us. As we write in this way, we find something that discloses the slightest silhouette. We do not know what this is. Perhaps one's own infantile, narrow-minded desires, or an object quite near, but ultimately something that is neither continues to glint and glimmer. It's as though we might be able to touch it if we reach a little further. That yearning makes me keep writing poems. We are stranded all alone, in this fog of perpetual suspension and impossibility.

3

So to write that something is or isn't must be no different from saying one wishes it is or isn't.

Though we know all this is useless, we write, in this space where we cannot gain freedom or meet the true object. Keeping the faith that one day, it will be so.

Let there be light.

Saying so repeatedly is declaration and testimony and prayer, the archetype of all writing acts.

All those phantasms, replicas, shadows created by what is written, those countless false rays we create because we are human: in their midst we yearn even as we fail over and over. With closed eyes, directing our hearts to the object we haven't seen and cannot see, we continue to take the position of prayer.

Putting aside all the stories repeated, reversed, and colliding in this short essay, I want to leave behind that single position. So I say it once more. I merely write–within that darkness and impossibility.

POET'S ESSAY

Three Denials

1

Beauty is fundamentally sensed in a faraway object.

Something too close to oneself is not beautiful. No matter how beautiful someone might be, that person will not consider their reflection in the mirror beautiful. Therefore beauty is always a bit distanced from reality. The fact that beauty will not come into our grasp makes us mournful, and passionate as well.

An incident too close to oneself cannot be beautiful. One's own family's noble sacrifices cannot be beautiful, and when writing about a tragedy that occurred yesterday, it is impossible to make it a beautiful account. And this exactly is the reason for art's powerlessness.

At one point, the world generously accepted beauty's deceits, and even found inspiration in the deceits for new images of the world, but now our lives have become much too susceptible and complex. Now, I accept the countless signs of catastrophes that have appeared before us as imminent urgencies, things that cannot be bypassed or converted.

2

Kim Jongsam's poem "What Day Is It" is a dispassionate depiction of a hospital abandoned by its human occupants. Grasses grow thick in the space left behind by humans, and the poet describes their blue-green light as strewn about here and there like the souls of people. There is a single empty baby stroller there, an emphatic symbol of the world where humans have completely disappeared. This poem about vacant ruins is beautiful beyond belief, and even feels holy. In this world where even the sense of time has completely disappeared, the poem asks nonchalantly: what day is it today?

Kim, who carried the wounds of the Korean War all his life, must have dreamed of transcendence that could overcome that excruciating pain. Because he could not endure humans, because he could not watch yet another person die, he must have imagined a sacred world devoid of humans. Is it possible then to critique this beautiful world as an escapist dream? Even if it is escapist, would it be truly possible to call it unethical? In the past, there was a time when the fact that a person could sublimate their anguish into beauty was a radiant act of resistance against the world's brutality.

The moment I became captivated by poetry was one of these instances when beauty guilelessly revealed its transcendence. I was mesmerized by the light that spilled forth in the moment Chekhov's fiction exposed the grief of life in one fell swoop, and when Kim Jongsam's poem depicted a world teeming with absolute silence, I believed this was one of the most beautiful states poetry could reach. And I believed that those moments functioned and existed as meaningful antitheses of this world.

But one cannot write poems like these now. One should not write such poems. These thoughts are the compulsions I have as a poet.

3

Poet Jeong Han-ah's doctoral thesis, "Bread and tea: Gim Choon-soo's literature and politics after nonsense" offers a fascinating interpretation of Gim's work. The thesis contextualizes Gim's literary work with his involvement in politics during the Fifth Republic[*], (and as I understand it) actively addresses the dilemma faced by poets at present, when the relationship between literature and politics is to be formed anew.

This thesis ends in the following way:

"He doesn't need to endure anything at all. [...] One cannot definitively state whether what killed him was torture, his class status, historicism, or his phobia of isms, but it seems clear now that the effortless freedom he yearned for was no different from the freedom to live as if dead. Of one thing, he was right. The exceptionality of egotist philosophy

---

[*] The period of Chun Doo-hwan's de facto dictatorship from 1981 to 1988.

is neither defeated nor refuted by universalism, in any way. This is because within the ethics of egotist philosophy, the world is strictly separate from the self. The world—the totality of relations between the self and its others—can be handed off to the universalists, who think the world is an essential condition to life and the existence of the "I"; he would be better off drinking a cup of tea every day. That is, as long as he has not decided to go into politics."

Jung's article is a powerful critique of Gim's poetry and life, this poet who has maintained a peculiar ahistorical stance in his writing. Through this terrific dissertation, Jung seems to be saying an indirect farewell to the value of "useless literature", a belief long held within Korean literary history. The idea that literature would save our lives, not despite but because it is useless, was a crucial principle within Korean literature. But the era in which the uselessness of art symbolized dissent has ended, and many poets and artists are plagued by the anxiety that their poetry's uselessness merely bolsters the stability of the establishment. Jung's critique of Gim Choon-soo would ultimately have also been a ruthless critique of Jung herself.

4

One of my most oft-recurring thoughts lately is about how I might stop feeling hostile toward beauty. When I think about beauty, I feel like I'm committing a sin. Thinking about beauty feels like an act of deceit. When I feel sad looking at something beautiful, I am disappointed by my sadness.

However, there's actually no reason to be hostile

toward beauty. This is (as always) a refraction of my enmity toward myself, a disguise for my own powerlessness. It's not as if what I need to do has changed much. As a poet, I write poems, and at times, as a citizen, I think about how the future of communities can be made sustainable. As my poet-self and citizen-self continue to live in check of each other, as I continue to write poems while despising beauty yet remaining unable to depart from it, perhaps the arenas in which poetry can be useful will expand. If not, life will go on somehow. It's hard to think of anything that makes me as afraid or flustered as a life that keeps going, but that of all things can't be helped, can it.

COMMENTARY

A Future that Has Already Arrived

Kang Seong-eun (Poet)

One time Inchan and a few poets including myself went to a zoo in Gwacheon. At the zoo, Inchan looked excited, like a frantic kid. He said he usually goes to the zoo once a year. He would have been at the zoo the year before, and the year before that too. We saw eagles and flamingos and peacocks. Why are there only flocks of birds that don't fly crowding my memories of that day? Inchan guided us around the zoo with ease and gave an explanation about the peacock's wings as well but I don't remember exactly what was said. I remember we were at the zoo until sundown and left as it got dark. As we walked out of the zoo while the darkness descended I heard some animal cries that seemed melancholy somehow. I wondered whether the animals felt relief or loneliness and isolation in that place emptied of humans.

Animals and the zoo often appear in Hwang's poems. In this collection too, Hwang seems to understand the speech of pigs, ducks, or rabbits; their silent gestures; the sadness of a bear that does not hibernate. What stance does the heart take in understanding? Even more, how is it possible to not "[know] what it [is], but still / [understand] something" ("Traffic")?

One takes a walk
Another falls in the water

People keep wandering the outskirts of the park

and that is the life of moderns I see I understand

But this has no relation to understanding I
understand that as well

—Excerpt from "You Have Reached the End of the Future"

There are people who keep wandering the
outskirts of the park during lunch. One takes a
walk, one falls in the water, a couple says their
farewells, and they are all tied up. This is the
life of the modern human. But the scene of the
person who has fallen in the water walking out
of it is also the life of a modern. He will walk out
of the water and still wander the outskirts of the
park. Because of the conditions of life in which
he cannot go anywhere but the park, he becomes
a sad modern-day human who must understand
without knowing. What is the future to a modern-

day human? Perhaps something like Heaven that has left and doesn't return, no matter how long one waits in front of its door one has only reached after a long journey ("Before the Law"). The person who walks out of the water will not have met Heaven in the water either.

Once again, how is it possible to understand something without knowing it ("Traffic")? To say one understands is to take a stance of acceptance. Therefore instead of resigning or giving up, he has decided on cold acceptance. Of the fact that one cannot go somewhere other than the park. The fact that this here, where he is walking, is the future.

I'm reminded of the poet's words from a past collection: "Love, that sort of thing you can just give anybody". The firm, spirited tone made me laugh as soon as I read it. If love is something you can just give anybody, I think love is also in this park called the future. Rowing a boat with a lover on a quiet, mist-shrouded lake, finding oneself alone on the fog-filled lake where the lover's laughter and the sound of rowing has disappeared and the beloved's face cannot be seen ("Jigukchong Jigukchong")—this too is a future that one has arrived at and must accept. This future is not a temporality that has yet to arrive but a specific time and place, not something far off but a certain sensation that is here and now, in front of one's eyes.

The moment morning light descends and lingers at the dining table
    and everything is set in place like a still life painting or a shot from a movie

—Excerpt from "Waking Hour"

Moments like these are sensed not only in this poem, but depicted in all poems by Hwang Inchan. At once, time has stopped and sounds stilled in this space where even the reader feels like they should hold their breath. At this moment, a strange poetic tautness appears, and silence slowly turns into an omen. But this transformation occurs so slowly that upon looking around, the reader finds themselves in the eye of a storm. As if one has become a modern-day human without knowing, as if one has already arrived at the future that used to feel so far off.

The way we walked around the zoo those years ago, the way the animals in the zoo's cages looked resemble the way people wander the park. I think of asking Inchan if he's been to the zoo lately, and stop myself. These days, you can't really go anywhere easily. The animals must still be there, but when we go there again sometime the animals and we too will be living as different beings compared to the past. I think of "places we'd been but wanted to visit again, things we wanted to see there again" ("Light"), but here is the future that has already arrived. Inside the future, there is someone who says he understands what one will never know. There, we all are.

WHAT THEY SAY ABOUT HWANG INCHAN

POET

He will go further. Toward the deep, hidden side of negativity that began in *Washing a Myna* and was reached in *Heeji's World*. For he is, as I said, an intelligent and kind, cheerful child. He won't give up on the world of animals that are birds and dogs, the 'Heeji' of the "her"s through his language. He will "revel" in the state of mind that unfolds via negativity and simplicity, that act of pure and implicit language. This is what Hwang Inchan has declared for himself as the name of the poet, and the fate of the one who truly wants to write. Therefore what must be read from him is the inevitability of the world he is constructing. The other side of the negativity and cynicism those innocent languages must take on to reveal themselves. That is to say, the cheerful exercises of the secretive intention that desperately seek to form through not speaking.

Kim Jeong-hyeon, "You will now become a pleasure 'unknown'",
2018 Donga New Writers Award

When the sentence "I think" pierces Hwang Inchan's poetry, it begins at the attitude or interest of the "I" that ceaselessly gazes at the poetic objects, and comes to pierce the surface of the object via seeing and ultimately "losing" the "I" in that empty space. ("Look too long and you'll lose your soul", from "Last of a Species") What is left then is a world like an unidentifiable "husk". His poetry shows that the capacity to correspond to something by steadily looking at it is based upon the strange sensation that abandons the initial unyielding world of the "I" and pierces the object's skin to form a more voluminous world; therefore what might be called "I" disappears and a space where merely the voice of the "I" echoes ever so faintly is created in the name of poetry. Thus the sentence "I think" in Hwang's poetry is illuminated with a new grammar of observation.

Kim Nayoung, "A New Observance: on Hwang Inchan's Washing a Myna", Changbi Spring 2013

Hwang often uses the word "poetry" in his poems. Though he self-deprecatingly mutters, "Poets who don't have anything to write about write about poems all the time" ("Yoga Class"), the "poem" that he refers to when he says "This poem begins within such dilemmas" or "I've decided to end this poem this way" ("Shattered") usually doesn't operate self-referentially "toward poetry" but appears as a subject speaking "toward life" and a "life-like" object. His poetry tries to resemble life. And so life regains the light of poetry. That light puts our oblivion at unease.

Kim Haengsook, " Repetition, Poetry that Snatches from the Everyday: on Hwang Inchan's Repetitions for Love", Munhakdongne Spring 2020.

K-POET
You Have Reached the End of the Future

Written by Hwang Inchan
Translated by Hoyoung Moon
Published by ASIA Publishers
Address 445, Hoedong-gil, Paju-si, Gyeonggi-do, Korea
Tel (8231).955.7958
Fax (8231).955.7956
Email bookasia@hanmail.net
Homepage Address www.bookasia.org

ISBN 979-11-5662-317-5 (set) | 979-11-5662-582-7 (04810)
First published in Korea by ASIA Publishers 2021

This book is published with the support of the Literature Translation Institute of Korea
(LTI Korea).